AESOP'S
FABLES

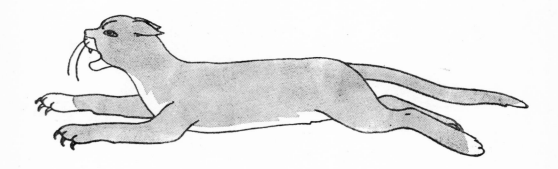

For Moral see page twenty-seven

A selection of

AESOP'S FABLES

Re-written especially for children by
BARBARA SANDERS
Illustrated by CHRISTOPHER SANDERS

THIS IS A CASTLE BOOK

Contents

THIS BOOK
        BELONGS TO

NAME...

ADDRESS..

AGE...

Contents

The Travellers and the Bear

The Travellers and the Bear

TWO men travelling through a forest together promised to help each other whatever danger threatened them. They had not gone far when a Bear rushed at them from some bushes. One man was a good climber, and quickly climbed a nearby tree, but the other, seeing that he had no chance alone against the Bear, fell flat on his back, and pretended to be dead. The Bear came up to him, sniffed at him, and thinking him dead went off into the wood again without hurting him. When he had gone, the other Traveller came down from his tree, and smilingly asked his companion what the Bear had said to him.

"For I could see," he said, "that he put his mouth close to your ear."

"He told me to tell you," replied the other, "that you were a great coward, and that in future I should not trust those who make fine promises, but will not stand by their friends in danger."

Moral

Don't trust fine promises unless you are sure of the person who makes them.

The Cock and the Jewel

The Cock and the Jewel

A COCK, scratching in the farm-yard for food for the hens, turned up a precious stone that shone and sparkled in the sun.

"Well," said the Cock, "I don't know what you are doing here. You are a very beautiful thing, and no doubt if your owner found you he would be delighted, but you are no good to me. I would rather have one grain of delicious barley than all the precious stones under the sun!"

Moral

Judge things by their true value.

The Fox and the Tiger

The Fox and the Tiger

AN Archer, hunting in the woods, was so successful with his arrows that he killed many of the wild animals. This frightened the rest so much that they ran into the densest part of the bushes to hide. At last the Tiger stood up, and pretending to be very brave, told the other animals not to be afraid anymore, but to rely on his courage, and he would attack the enemy on his own. While he was talking, and lashing his tail and tearing at the ground with his claws to impress the others, an arrow came and pierced his ribs. The Tiger howled with pain.

While he was trying to draw out the arrow with his teeth the Fox went up to him and asked, in surprise, whoever had the strength and courage to wound such a brave and mighty beast as the Tiger?

"Nay," said the Tiger, "I misjudged my enemy. It was that unbeatable man over there!"

Moral

Knowledge is power.

The Fowler and the Ringdove

The Fowler and the Ringdove

A FOWLER went into the woods to shoot a Ringdove with his bow and arrow, when an adder that he had trodden upon in the grass, turned and stung him. As the poison spread, and the Fowler realized that he was dying, he said: "That is true justice! I was planning to kill, and something else killed me!"

Moral

If you make trouble you will get into trouble.

The Wolf and the Crane

The Wolf and the Crane

A WOLF one day had a bone stuck in his throat which was very painful, so he went howling about the place begging every animal he met to take the bone out, and promising a reward to anyone that would do so. The Crane, tempted by the thought of the reward, made the Wolf swear that he would keep his promise, and then put his long neck into the greedy creature's throat and picked out the bone. Then he asked for his reward.

The Wolf looked at him disdainfully and said: "How can you be so stupid? I had your head in my mouth, and could easily have bitten it off, but I let you take it away without doing so, and now you are not contented!"

Moral

Do not run silly risks.

The Fox and the Crocodile

The Fox and the Crocodile

DURING an argument between a Fox and a Crocodile about good birth and noble descent, the Crocodile boasted about his ancient and noble family. The Fox smiled, and replied: "Friend, you don't need to speak of your family! You carry the marks of your lowly origin on your skin!"

Moral

Foolish boasting only makes people laugh at us.

The Porcupine and the Snakes

The Porcupine and the Snakes

A PORCUPINE, looking for shelter, found some Snakes living in a cave. He asked if he could join them, and they at once said that he could do so. When he went in with them, however, his sharp prickly quills were so uncomfortable that they very quickly asked him to go out again.

"Certainly not!" said the Porcupine. "Anybody who doesn't like this place can leave it. Personally, I am comfortable."

Moral

If you choose your friends thoughtlessly you may lose everything.

The Fox and the Lion

The Fox and the Lion

THE first time the Fox saw the Lion, he was so terrified that he lay down at his feet, and nearly died of fright. The second time, he was not so frightened, and stood and looked at the Lion. The third time, he was not frightened at all, but said "Good morning!" and stopped and talked to the Lion.

Moral

Familiarity breeds contempt.

The Miser Burying his Gold

The Miser Burying his Gold

A RICH man once sold all his estates, melted all the Gold with which he was paid into a large piece, and buried it in the earth. He went to see it every day, and these visits attracted the attention of a thief, who went to the place one night, found the Gold, and stole it. The Miser was nearly mad with grief when he discovered his loss, but a neighbour said to him :

" Why are you so upset ? You did not spend the Gold, so it was of no use to you ; it was simply the feeling that you had it. Get a stone. Pretend that is the Gold, and bury it. It will be just as useful ! "

Moral

The greedy value possessions so much that they never gain anything of real value.

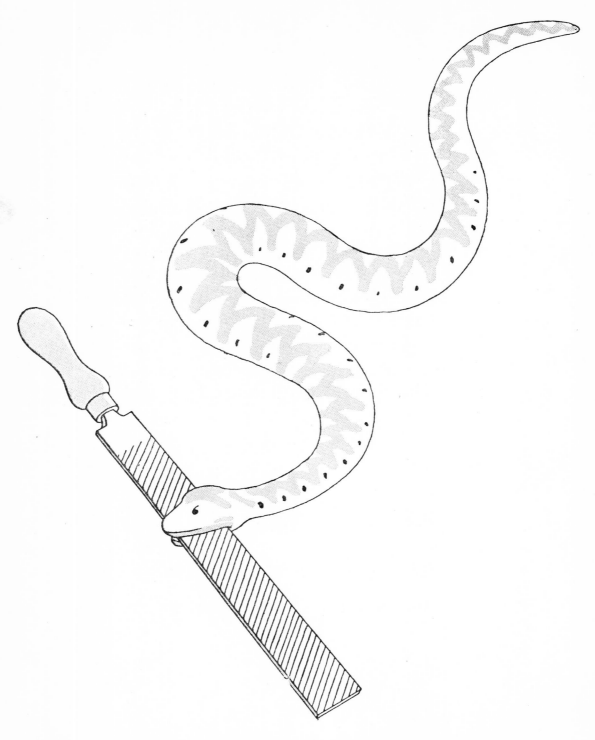

The Viper and the File

The Viper and the File

A VIPER went into a smiths' shop, and, feeling hungry, looked about for something to eat. The only thing he could find was a file, which he started gnawing greedily.

The File, however, spoke gruffly to him, and told him that he had better stop, as he could not expect to get much out of something who could himself, if necessary, bite iron and steel.

Moral

Do not try to do the things you know you are not capable of doing.

The Ass in the Lion's Skin

The Ass in the Lion's Skin

AN Ass found a Lion's skin, dressed himself up in it, and went among the flocks and herds frightening the animals out of their wits.

At last he met his master, and tried to frighten him, but the man, seeing the long ears sticking out, knew him at once and, taking a stick, beat him until he realized that although he was dressed in a Lion's skin, he was really only an Ass !

Moral

Don't pretend to be what you are not.

Jupiter and the Herdsman

Jupiter and the Herdsman

A HERDSMAN lost a calf, and could not find it anywhere, so he prayed to the God Jupiter.

"Great Jupiter," he said, "if you will show me who has stolen my calf, I will sacrifice a kid for you."

He had hardly finished praying when the thief stood before him. It was a lion. The man at once fell upon his knees and prayed again!

"Great Jupiter, I have not forgotten my promise, but now that you have shown me the thief, I will sacrifice a bull instead of a kid if you will only make him go away again!"

Moral

It is not good for us to have everything we wish for.

The Tortoise and the Eagle

The Tortoise and the Eagle

A TORTOISE was tired of always being on the ground, and wanted to fly in the air, so he let it be known that if any bird would take him up and show him the world from the air, he would tell him, as a reward, where many precious stones were hidden in a cave.

The Eagle, hearing of the reward, said he would take the Tortoise up, and lifting him in his claws, carried him up a great height. When there, he asked the Tortoise to tell him where the reward could be found, but the Tortoise could not tell him.

Angry at being deceived, the Eagle dropped the Tortoise onto the rocks below where he was dashed to pieces, and the Eagle made a meal of him !

Moral

Do not make a promise unless you know you can keep it.

The Swallow and the Crow

The Swallow and the Crow

THE Swallow and the Crow were arguing about which of them was the more beautiful.

"You," said the Crow, "are only beautiful in the winter. I am beautiful all the year round."

Moral

That which lasts longest is strongest.

The Husbandman and the Stork

The Husbandman
and the Stork

A HUSBANDMAN set a net in his fields to catch the cranes and geese who would eat his newly sown barley. He caught several of both, and also a Stork. The Stork pleaded not to be killed, pointing out that he was neither crane nor goose, but only a poor harmless Stork who was very good to his old parents; feeding them and, if necessary, carrying them from one place to another.

"That may be," said the Husbandman, "but I have caught you in bad company and committing the same crime, so you must expect to suffer the same punishment!"

Moral

Bad friends do you no good.

The Cat and the Cock

The Cat and the Cock

THE Cat made up his mind to make a meal of the Cock, so he took him by surprise one morning, and when he had caught him, asked him if he knew of any reason why he should not be killed. The Cock replied that he made himself very useful to man by crowing in the early morning, and waking him in time for his work.

"That is exactly what I complain of!" cried the Cat. "You make such a terrible noise that nobody can sleep, and people will not put up with these interruptions to their rest. Your own words show that you are obviously not fit to live."

Moral

A person who wants to do wrong can easily find an excuse for doing it.

The Fox and the Goat

The Fox and the Goat

A FOX fell into a well, and could not manage to climb out again. Presently a Goat came along, wanting a drink, and asked the Fox if the water was good.

"Very!" said the Fox. "In fact it is so good that I'm afraid I have drunk too much, and shall be ill!"

The Goat at once jumped into the water, and the Fox, leaping on his horns, jumped out, leaving the Goat in the well to get out as best he could.

Moral

Treat your friends as they deserve
to be treated.

The Hare and the Tortoise

The Hare and the Tortoise

A HARE laughed at a Tortoise because of his slowness, and boasted of her own speed in running.

"Very well," replied the Tortoise, "let us have a race. I will run with you for five miles for a wager, and the Fox shall act as umpire."

"Agreed," said the Hare, and off they started. The Hare outran the Tortoise so much that she made fun of the whole thing, and decided to take a nap in a clump of ferns, thinking that when the Tortoise came past, she could easily overtake him.

Meanwhile the Tortoise came jogging along slowly but steadily, and passing the Hare, who still slept because she was over-confident, won the race easily.

Moral

More haste, less speed.

The Woman and the Hen

The Woman and the Hen

A WOMAN once had a Hen that laid an egg for her every day. This made the Old Woman think that if she gave the bird twice as much food it would lay two eggs a day, instead of one, so she doubled its allowance of barley.

Unfortunately the extra food made the Hen grow so fat that it stopped laying altogether!

Moral

When things are going well, don't spoil them by being greedy.

The Astrologer and the Traveller

The Astrologer
and the Traveller

AN Astrologer was so busy gazing at the stars that he fell into a ditch while walking along. A passerby saw him, and said :

"Friend, you should learn from this to let the stars go their own way, while you look more carefully where you are going !"

Moral

Mind your own business.

The Hawk and the Nightingale

The Hawk and the Nightingale

A NIGHTINGALE sitting in a tree sang so sweetly and shrilly that she attracted the attention of a hungry Hawk, who flew down, seized the Nightingale in his claws, and told her he was going to kill her. The little bird begged him not to do anything so cruel and unworthy.

"I have never done you any wrong," said the Nightingale, "and I am much too small for such a large bird as yourself. Go and catch a bigger bird who will be more worthy of you, and will make a better meal."

"Nothing you can say will change my mind," replied the Hawk. "I have caught nothing all day until I found you. What a fool I should be to let you go in the hopes of catching something bigger!"

Moral

A bird in the hand is worth two in the bush.

The Two Cocks Fighting

The Two Cocks Fighting

TWO Cocks had a fight to decide which should be King of the Farmyard. The winner, very pleased with himself, flew upon the fence, crowing and flapping his wings, and so attracted the attention of a passing eagle. The bird flew down and carried him off, which left the defeated Cock head of the farmyard.

Moral

Too much pride will be your downfall.

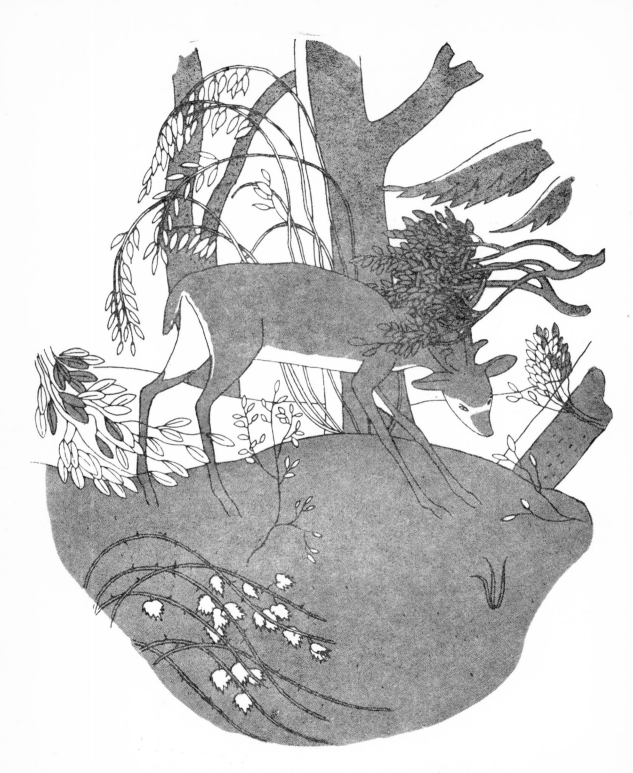

The Stag drinking at the Pool

The Stag Drinking at the Pool

A STAG, drinking at a Pool, saw the reflection of himself in the water, and was very pleased with it.

"How beautiful I am!" he said. "What splendid antlers I have! It is a pity that my feet are not as lovely as my antlered head."

Suddenly he heard the sound of a huntsman and his hounds, but by using his nimble feet the Stag was soon away from his enemies.

Not long after this, on going amongst some dense trees, he caught his antlers among the branches, and being unable to move, the hounds this time caught up with him, and pulled him down.

" Stupid creature that I am !" he said to himself. " These antlers that I was so proud of have caused my downfall, while the feet that I despised might have saved me !"

Moral

*Beauty can be a very powerful gift,
but it can be a dangerous one.*

The Fox and the Hare appeal to Jupiter

The Fox and the Hare
Appeal to Jupiter

THE Fox and the Hare both prayed to Jupiter; the Fox asking for the speed of the Hare, and the Hare for the cunning of the Fox.

In answer to their prayers Jupiter told them that every creature had some advantage not possessed by the others, and it would not be fair to give all the advantages to one animal.

Moral

No creature should wish to be like another, because each was given its own particular gifts.

The Wolf, the Lamb, and the Goat

The Wolf, the Lamb, and the Goat

A WOLF one day saw a Lamb being mothered by a Goat.

"Child, you are making a mistake," he said. "This is not your mother, your real mother is over there," and he pointed to a flock of sheep in the distance.

"Perhaps you are right," said the Lamb, "but this Goat has always looked after me, and even denied her own Kids so that I should not go hungry. I have had all the food and kindness from her that have kept me alive so far, and I shall always look upon her as my mother."

Moral

Parents who do not look after their children deserve no consideration, but kindness deserves credit.

The Eagle and the Crow

The Eagle and the Crow

AN Eagle flew down from his nest on the top of a mountain, and fastening his claws in the back of a lamb, took it back to his lofty home. A Crow, seeing what the Eagle did, determined to copy him, so it flew down on to the back of a ram, and fastening its claws in its wool, started chattering while trying to fly. The noise attracted the shepherd, who caught the Crow easily because its feet were tangled in the ram's wool, and gave it to his boys to play with.

Moral

Most of our troubles are our own fault.

The Old Hound

The Old Hound

AN old Hound who had, in his time, been of great service to his master, became old and feeble and no longer useful or of any use. While they were hunting a stag one day, however, he happened to be near it when it fell, and seized it by one leg; but the Hound's teeth were old and decayed, and could not hold the stag, which struggled free, and escaped. The master was very angry at this, and was just going to beat him, when the old creature apologized, and said:

"Do not strike your old servant, master. It is not my intentions that are failing, but my strength and speed. If I do not please you now, I beg you remember what I have done in the past!"

Moral

Never forget anything which has been done for you.

The Shepherd's Boy

The Shepherd's Boy

A SHEPHERD Boy once kept his Sheep on a common next to a field where labourers worked. He was a mischievous boy, and would often call out "the Wolf! the Wolf!" just for the fun of fetching the men from their work in the field. When they found what the Boy was doing, they decided not to take any notice of him in future.

Soon after this a Wolf really did come, and the Boy called in earnest. No notice was taken of his cry, and the sheep were eaten up by the Wolf.

Moral

If you tell lies, even in fun, you will be very sorry afterwards.

The Crow and the Pitcher

The Crow and the Pitcher

A THIRSTY Crow looking for water, saw a pitcher in the distance, and flew joyfully towards it. The pitcher certainly had water in it, but it was so near the bottom, that no matter how he strained and struggled, the Crow could not reach it.

Then he tried to overturn the pitcher, so that he could at least have a little of the water when it spilt·on the ground; but he was not strong enough to do this.

Just then he saw some pebbles lying near, so he picked them up, one at a time, and dropped them into the pitcher. As the pebbles filled the pitcher, the water gradually rose until it was level with the top, and the Crow was able to drink at last.

Moral

You can often do more by thinking than you can by using your strength.

The Ox and the Frog

The Ox and the Frog

AN Ox, grazing in a field, put his foot among several young Frogs, and accidentally killed one of them. When their mother came home, the little Frogs told her what had happened, and said that the animal that killed their brother was the largest they had ever seen in their lives.

"Was it as big as this?" said the old Frog, swelling herself up.

"Oh! much bigger than that!" they cried.

"As big as this, then?" said the mother, swelling herself still more.

"Much, much bigger!" said the little Frogs. "If you swelled until you burst, you would not be as big!"

The old Frog tried again, and this time she swelled so much that she really did burst herself!

Moral

Be satisfied to be as you are.
Don't try to be like somebody else.

The Dog in the Manger

The Dog in the Manger

A DOG was lying on the hay in a manger, when an Ox, feeling hungry, came up and started to eat the hay. The Dog, however, was a bad-tempered, selfish creature, and would not let him touch it.

This made the Ox feel very annoyed, and he said in an angry voice: "You are a greedy, unpleasant creature! You can't eat the hay yourself, and you won't let anyone eat it who can!"

Moral

Live and let live,

or

Do what you yourself want, but let other people do the same.

The Horse and the Lion

The Horse and the Lion

A LION saw a fat young colt, and wanted to eat him, but did not know how to catch him. At last he had an idea. He told everyone that he was a doctor who had had experience in foreign countries, and so could cure every kind of illness in any animal.

The Horse, however, was certain this was a trick, and determined to get the better of the Lion. He pretended he had no suspicions, and went to him, saying that he had a very painful thorn in his foot which was making him lame, and would he help him. The Lion agreed to do this, and asked to see the foot. The Horse lifted up one of his hind feet, and while the Lion was pretending to look for the thorn the Horse gave him such a kick in the face, that he was stunned, and fell upon the ground. Then the Horse trotted away very pleased with himself for having successfully tricked someone who had meant to kill him.

Moral

Too much craftiness defeats itself.

The Fox and the Stork

The Fox and the Stork

A FOX invited a Stork to dinner, and decided to play a practical joke on him. He served nothing but some soup in a wide, shallow dish. The Fox, of course, could lap up the soup quite easily, but the Stork could only dip the tip of his long bill in the dish, and so got practically nothing.

A few days later the Stork invited the Fox to dinner. All he served was some minced meat in a glass jar, so tall and narrow that all the Fox could do was to pick up the pieces dropped by the Stork while he was eating!

The Fox was very angry at first, but when it was time for him to go home, he admitted that he had only been treated as he deserved, and that he should not be annoyed at something which he himself had first done.

Moral

If you play practical jokes you must expect other people to do the same.

The Wolf in Sheep's Clothing

The Wolf in Sheep's Clothing

A WOLF dressed himself in the skin of a sheep and, so disguised, was able to go among the flock, and kill and eat many of them.

At last the shepherd found him out, and to punish him, hanged him from a nearby tree. Some other shepherds, passing by, stopped and exclaimed:

"Surely you are not hanging a sheep?"

"No," replied the first shepherd, "but I always hang a Wolf if I find it in sheep's clothing." And when he showed them what he was really hanging, the other shepherds agreed that the punishment was just.

Moral

The advantage gained by lying only lasts until the truth is found out.

The Lion and the Mouse

The Lion and the Mouse

A LION lay down under a tree to rest, and while he slept some little mice ran over his nose and woke him up. He jumped up and put his paw on one of them, and was just going to kill it when it pleaded for mercy, saying that it was beneath the Lion's dignity to kill such a tiny creature. The Lion, on thinking it over, agreed, and let the grateful little Mouse go.

Not long after the Lion was caught by hunters, and finding himself tied with ropes, started to howl and roar hideously. The little Mouse heard him, and recognizing him, told him not to be afraid; then with his sharp little teeth he gnawed through the ropes that held the Lion and set him free.

Moral

The least may help the greatest.

The Eagle and the Arrow

The Eagle and the Arrow

AN Eagle, who sat on a rock watching for his prey, had the bad luck to be hit by an arrow. This arrow was feathered with one of the Eagle's own feathers, and recognizing it as he sank, wounded, to the ground, the Eagle felt this his bitterest pain; that his own feather had helped bring about his death.

Moral

The unpleasant things that happen to us always seem worse if we can be blamed for them.

The Lion, the Fox, and the Wolf

The Lion, the Fox, and the Wolf

THE Lion, the King of the Beasts, had grown old and ill, and all the beasts of the forest came to see him, except the Fox.

Now the Wolf and the Fox, two sly creatures, were always tricking each other, and the Wolf saw his chance to play a trick on the Fox. He went to the Lion, and said :

"Your Majesty, it is nothing but pride and insolence that stops the Fox coming to see how you are."

Fortunately for himself the Fox heard this, and at once went and bowed before the Lion.

"Sir," he said, "I think I am as loyal a subject as any of those who have been to see you, and I have certainly taken as much trouble as any of them to help you ; for I have been searching everywhere for a cure for your illness ; and I have found one !"

"Tell me at once what it is," cried the Lion.

"Nothing but to skin a live Wolf," replied the Fox, "and to wrap yourself in the warm skin."

The Wolf was standing near while he spoke, and the Fox, with a sneer, then advised him not to try to put a prince against his subjects, but to give him wise and peaceful advice.

Moral

Unkind actions come back upon us.

The Two Frogs

The Two Frogs

A LAKE in which two Frogs had lived for a long time dried up one very hot summer, and the Frogs had to leave it, and look for water somewhere else. As they went along, they came to a very deep well, with a lot of water in it.

"Good!" exclaimed one Frog. "We need not go any farther! This well is cool and deep, and will be a very comfortable place in which to live. Let us jump in!"

"Wait," said the other Frog, "and think for a minute. If this water were to dry up, how should we get out again?"

Moral

Easier in than out.

A Gnat Challenges a Lion

A Gnat Challenges a Lion

A LION was roaring proudly in the forest when a gnat flew up to him, and told him not to be so noisy and domineering.

"I am not afraid of your teeth and claws," said the Gnat, "I defy you! Let us fight at once." And he flew up the nostril of the Lion and stung him so badly that the Lion tore himself with his own claws.

So the Gnat conquered the Lion. As he flew away, however, he got caught in a cobweb, and was eaten by a spider. As he died he thought how sad it was that he who had conquered a Lion should be beaten by an insect.

Moral

Despise not small things.

The Ape and the Fox

The Ape and the Fox

THE Ape met the Fox one day, and asked him to give him some of the hairs from his tail to cover himself, as he had no tail, and so was exposed to all kinds of weather.

"And you friend, have so much tail that some of it even drags in the mud."

The Fox replied that he didn't know about having too much tail, but if he had, he would rather sweep the ground with his tail all his life than give up one hair to please an Ape.

Moral

Don't try to borrow, then you won't be disappointed if you are refused.

The Sheep and the Crow

The Sheep and the Crow

A CROW sat one day chattering on the back of a Sheep.

"Had I been a dog," said the Sheep, "you would not have dared to treat me like this!"

"I know that," said the Crow, "but I have sense enough to know with whom I am dealing. I can be as quiet as anything with quarrelsome people, but as troublesome as I like with people who will put up with it!"

Moral

If you never stand up for yourself, you will not be thought much of.

The Snake and the Crab

The Snake and the Crab

A SNAKE and a Crab became friends, and the Crab, who was a very straight-forward person, advised the Snake to give up his deceitful ways, and become honest. The Snake, however, refused to do this, and the Crab, seeing that the case was hopeless and that his friend would never reform, strangled the Snake as he slept. Looking at him as he lay stretched out straight and dead, the Crab said:

"Friend, this would never have happened to you if you had lived as straight as you died."

Moral

Good and evil cannot live and work together.

The Sow and the Wolf

The Sow and the Wolf

A WOLF, seeing a Sow lying in her sty with her litter of young pigs about her, wanted to make a meal of one of them, but did not know how to manage it. Eventually he tried to make friends with the Sow by saying to her: "How do you do, Mrs. Sow? Can I be of any help to you today? If you would like to go out for a breath of fresh air I shall be delighted to look after your children for you, and would take the greatest care of them."

"Thank you," said the Sow. "I fully appreciate your intentions, and to show you that I do, may I say that I would rather have your room than your company. You would oblige me by never letting me see your face again!"

Moral

Be careful not to take help from strangers, who may be deceiving you to help themselves.

The Lion and the Ass

The Lion and the Ass

A BOLD Ass once brayed insultingly at a Lion. At first the Lion snarled angrily and showed his teeth, but he soon stopped and said contemptuously: "Bray away! I shall take no notice. But remember this; it is only because you are such a poor creature that I do not kill you!"

Moral

It is better to ignore rudeness than to become annoyed by it.

The Fox and the Grapes

The Fox and the Grapes

A HUNGRY Fox came to a vineyard where some beautiful bunches of ripe grapes were hanging. They were nailed to a trellis, but so high up that, although he jumped until he was tired, the Fox could not reach them. At last he turned away, saying: "Anybody who wants the Grapes can have them! They are only green, sour things, so I will leave them alone!"

Moral

Do not wish for what you know you cannot have.

The Camel at First Sight

The Camel at First Sight

THE first time that people saw a Camel they all ran away from it in fear. Finding it did them no harm, they came back and looked at it. Presently they decided that it was a dull beast, so they harnessed it, put bundles and packs on its back, and treated it with the greater contempt.

Moral

We always fear things we know nothing about.

The Fox and the Crow

The Fox and the Crow

A CROW stole a piece of cheese, and in order to eat it flew into a high tree. A Fox saw this, so went and sat under the tree, and began to compliment the Crow on her beauty.

"I never noticed before what a delicate white your feathers are!" he exclaimed, "and what a fine and graceful shape your body is. I don't doubt that you have a fairly good voice, but if it is anything like your appearance, I don't know any bird that can compete with you!"

The Crow, flattered by all these compliments, strutted about and preened herself, but feeling that the Fox was a little doubtful of her voice, decided to reassure him as to its beauty, and opened her mouth to sing, dropping the cheese in the process.

This, of course, was what the Fox wanted, so he snapped up the cheese and ran off, laughing at the stupidity of the Crow.

Moral

Flattery finds favour.

The Two Pots

The Two Pots

TWO Pots, one of earthenware and one of brass, were standing together on the river bank, and were swept away by the current. The earthenware Pot looked very uneasy in case it should be broken, but the brass Pot told him not to be afraid, as he would take care of him.

"Oh!" cried the other Pot, "please keep as far away from me as you can! It is you I am afraid of! For whether the current knocks you against me, or me against you, I shall be the one to break, so please do not let us come near to each other!"

Moral

Do not make friends with everybody ; choose your friends carefully.

The Eagle and the Fox

The Eagle and the Fox

AN Eagle, looking for food for her young ones, saw a Fox's cub lying in the sun. Just as she swooped and seized it the mother Fox came up and begged the Eagle to pity the distress of a mother, and spare her child. But the Eagle took no notice, and carried the young Fox to her nest high up in a tree where she thought she was safe.

The Fox, however, was cunning, and running to a fire nearby, seized a burning stick in her mouth, and started to climb towards the Eagle's nest. The Eagle, afraid for her nest and her children, begged the the Fox to stop, and at once returned the baby Fox safely to the ground.

Moral

Measure for measure,

or

You must expect to be treated as you treat others.

The Old Man and his Sons

The Old Man and his Sons

AN Old Man had several Sons who would quarrel with each other despite anything that he could do to stop them. So one day he ordered a bundle of sticks to be brought him, and then called his Sons to him, and told them all to try to break the bundle. They each tried, but were unsuccessful. The sticks were so closely bound together that it was impossible for any man to break them.

Then the father had the bundle untied, and gave each Son a single stick, telling him to try to break that. This he did easily.

Then the Old Man spoke to them and said, "Now, my Sons, you see the strength of unity. If you would all stand together, nobody could harm you, but if you keep quarrelling among yourselves, you will be an easy prey for your enemies, because you deprive yourselves of the strength of unity."

Moral

People who will not work together cannot succeed.

The Mischievous Dog

The Mischievous Dog

THERE was once a Dog who was so bad tempered and mischievous that his master had to hang a heavy piece of wood round its neck, to stop it running at people, and biting them. The stupid dog mistook the wood for a medal, and grew so conceited about it that he looked down in scorn upon all other dogs, and refused to have anything to do with them. But one wise old dog among the others pointed out to him that he had nothing to be proud of, because the wood that hung round his neck was there as a mark of disgrace, and not of honour.

Moral

" Oh, wad some pow'r the giftie gie us,
To see oursels as others see us !"

or

What a pity we cannot see ourselves
as other people see us.

The Fox and the Cock

The Fox and the Cock

A FOX, passing a farmyard one day, was caught in the trap that had been set for him. The Cock, seeing what had happened, crept as near as he dare, upon which the Fox spoke to him in a very deceitful way.

"You see, friend, what has happened to me," he said, "and it is really all your fault. I heard you crow as I was passing, and wanted to ask you how you did it before I went home, and as I was coming to see you I got caught like this. So I beg you, either to fetch me a knife to cut the string that ties me, or not to tell anyone I am here until I have bitten through.

The Cock, however, saw how things were. He flew away to tell the farmer, who at once went and killed the Fox before he could escape.

Moral

Help those who deserve it.

The Bear and the Beehive

The Bear and the Beehive

A BEAR climbed over a fence into a garden where bees were kept, and began to plunder the hives, and steal the honey.

The Bees were very angry, and in order to revenge themselves, attacked him all together. They were not able to pierce his thick skin, but they stung his eyes and nose so much that the irritation made the Bear tear the skin over his ears with his own claws, which fully punished him for stealing the Bees' honey!

Moral

Do not despise the little things in life, you may suffer for it.

The Leopard and the Fox

The Leopard and the Fox

THE Leopard one day was boasting of the beauty of his spots, and saying that even the Lion should not be superior to him, as he had not nearly such a beautiful skin. As for all the other animals, he treated them with complete disdain.

The Fox, however, went up to the Leopard and told him in no uncertain terms that he was much mistaken to put such a value upon himself, as intelligent people did not judge character by outside appearances, but by the good qualities of the other person's mind.

Moral

Handsome is that handsome does

or

It is no good looking beautiful if
you do not behave well.

The Lion and the Four Bulls

The Lion and the Four Bulls

FOUR Bulls in a field always kept near to one another, and fed together. A Lion, watching them from a distance, wanted to eat them, but while he could have attacked any one of them alone, he dared not risk it whilst they were all together, because he knew they would defeat him. So he thought of a plan. He started unkind rumours about the Bulls, and spread them about as though they had been talking about each other. The Bulls heard the rumours, and became so distrustful of each other that they separated, and each fed by himself. The Lion then fell upon each one in turn, and ate them all up.

Moral

We are stronger when we stand together.

The Ass Eating Thistles

The Ass Eating Thistles

AN Ass, loaded with all kinds of good things to eat, was taking them to his master and the men working in the harvest field. On the way he saw a fine large thistle growing, and, feeling hungry, stopped to eat it. While doing so, he thought to himself: "Many people would think themselves very lucky to have some of the good things I carry on my back, but I would rather have this prickly thistle than everything I carry put together."

Moral

That which is one man's meat
is another man's poison,

or

Not everybody likes the same thing.

The Fox in the Well

The Fox in the Well

A FOX fell into a well and had great difficulty in keeping his head above water. He clung to the side with his claws, and when presently a Wolf came to the well, the Fox begged him to go and get a rope and help him out. The Wolf stood and looked at him, and said: "Poor Fox! I am sorry for you. However did you get in there?"

"Friend," said the Fox, "it is very kind of you to be sorry for me, but that will not get me out of here! If you wish me well, don't stand there, but go and find something that will help me out."

Moral

To say well is good, but to do well is better

The Dog and the Shadow

The Dog and the Shadow

A DOG, crossing a small stream with a piece of meat in his mouth, saw his shadow reflected in the clear water. Believing this to be another dog, who was carrying a larger piece of meat, he could not refrain from snatching at it. Far from gaining anything by his greedy action, he dropped the piece of meat he had in his mouth, and it sank to the bottom of the water, and was lost for good.

Moral

Don't lose what you have by wanting something you can't have.

The Wind and the Sun

The Wind and the Sun

THE North Wind and the Sun were arguing one day about which of them was the stronger. In the end they decided to test each other by seeing which of them could first make a traveller take off his coat.

The North Wind began, and he blew a very strong, cold blast, and added a sharp, driving shower of rain. This, and anything else he tried, instead of making the man take off his cloak, made him wrap it even more **tightly** round himself to keep out the cold.

Then the Sun started. He came from behind a thick watery cloud, drove the cold mists from the sky, and shone his hottest rays onto the head of the poor weather-beaten Traveller. The rays were so hot that the man grew faint, took off his cloak, and, unable to stand the Sun any longer, went to some nearby trees for shade.

Moral

Gentle words work better than hard ones.

The Wolf and the Lamb

The Wolf and the Lamb

ONE hot day a Wolf and a Lamb arrived at the same time to drink from a stream that ran down the side of a mountain. The Wolf was on the high ground, and the Lamb some way farther down the stream.

The Wolf, however, felt quarrelsome, and asked the Lamb what he meant by disturbing the water, and making it so that he could not drink it. The Lamb, frightened by the Wolf's angry voice, answered that he did not see how that could be, as the water which he drank ran from the Wolf to him, and so could not be disturbed higher up the stream.

"Perhaps so," said the Wolf, "but you are an unpleasant person, and I have been told that you said nasty things about me behind my back about six months ago!"

"That cannot be true," exclaimed the Lamb, "for I was not born then!"

The Wolf could not argue that point, and was furious; snarling, and foaming at the mouth, he went towards the Lamb.

"Well," he shouted, "if it wasn't you, it was your father, which comes to the same thing!" and he seized the poor Lamb, and ate it all up.

Moral

A wicked man will always find an excuse for doing wrong.

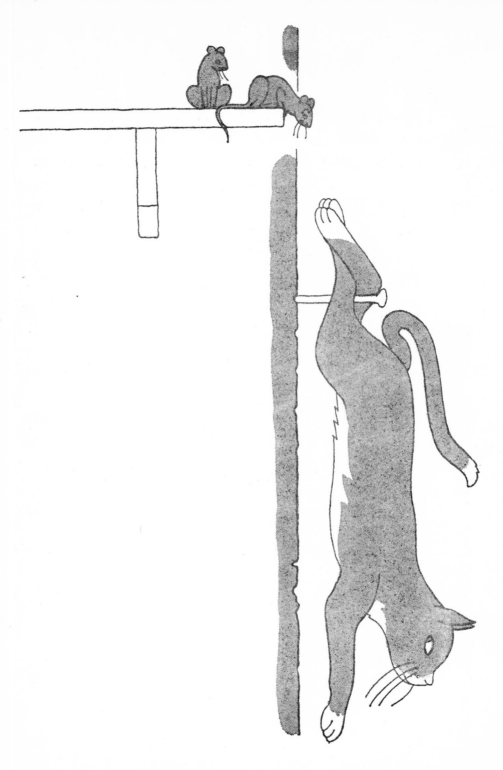

The Cat and the Mice

The Cat and the Mice

A HOUSE was once so over-run with Mice that the owner was obliged to get a cat, who killed and ate some of them each day The Mice soon saw what was happening, and had a meeting to decide what should be done, and after a lot of discussion, decided that no mouse was to go down below the top shelf. This plan worked very well for the Mice, but the Cat, hungry because she had no Mice to eat, prowled round the house wondering what she could do. Eventually she decided on a plan herself. She hung by her hind legs from a peg in the wall, and pretended she was dead, hoping that the mice would come down to the ground again. But she was disappointed. One wise old mouse peeped over the edge of the shelf at her hanging there, and said :

"There you are, are you? Well, you may stop there! I would not trust myself near you even if you were stuffed with straw!"

Moral

We learn by experience.

The Ass, the Ape, and the Mole

The Ass, the Ape,
and the Mole

AN Ass and an Ape were grumbling together; the Ass complaining that he had no horns, and the Ape that he had no tail.

"Be quiet," said a Mole who was listening, "stop grumbling and be grateful for what you have. We poor moles, who are quite blind, are worse off than any of you!"

Moral

We should never complain as long as there are others worse off than ourselves.

The Fox without a Tail

The Fox without a Tail

A FOX, caught in a trap by his tail, was glad to escape by leaving his tail behind. After a time, however, he began to realize what disgrace such a loss would be to him, and he almost wished that he had died, rather than lose his tail. Eventually he decided to make the best of it, so he called a meeting of Foxes, and made a long speech to them about the uselessness of tails in general, and of Foxes' tails in particular. He said that he had often thought that they would be better without them, and now he knew from personal experience, that that was true, for he had never enjoyed himself so much, or been so comfortable as he was now that he had no tail; and he suggested that they all docked their tails to see for themselves.

One sly old Fox among them, however, saw through his ruse, and said with a smile, "I believe you found it very convenient to escape from a trap by leaving your tail behind, and if we are ever in the same position, we may do the same thing!"

Moral

Do not be led into mischief by the example of your friends.

The Town and Country Mouse

The Town and Country Mouse

A TOWN Mouse paid a visit to an old playfellow of his, an honest Country Mouse. The Country Mouse wanted to do everything possible to make his old friend comfortable and happy, so he put before him a meal of grey peas and bacon, a dish of fine oatmeal, some parings of new cheese, and, to crown all, a piece of delicious mellow apple for dessert; and in case his visitor should not have enough, he did not eat himself, but sat and nibbled a piece of wheat straw very busily. At last, The Town Mouse said:

"Old friend, may I speak plainly to you? How can you live here in this dirty, miserable hole with nothing but woods and fields, mountains and streams about you? Wouldn't you rather have learned conversation to the chirping of the birds, or the splendour of the Court to the rough living of the country? We are not as young as we were, and should make the most of the present, and spend it happily. Please—think no more about it, but come to Town with me."

At last he persuaded his friend, and towards evening the two mice set off for Town. About midnight they went into a very large house where a banquet had been held during the evening, and several bits and pieces were lying about on the floor. The Country Mouse was at once seated on a Persian Carpet, and then it was the Town Mouse's turn to entertain. This he did with great success, giving his friend all the delicate pieces, having first tasted them himself to make sure they were good; and the Country Mouse was delighted with his changed life and fortune.

Suddenly someone opened the door, and a large dog came barking into the room, causing the mice to run helter skelter all over the place in a very frightened way. The Country Mouse, in particular, was terrified, and when at last the noise and scurry had calmed down he said to his friend:

"Well, if this is your Town life, you are welcome to it! I shall go back as fast as possible to my poor, quiet hole, and my homely grey peas!"

Moral

It is better to put up with our troubles than take on others that we do not know about.

The Oak and the Reed

The Oak and the Reed

AN Oak tree growing beside a river was blown down by a gale of wind. As it was carried down the stream by the current, its branches brushed against the Reed growing near the bank. The Oak was surprised to see the Reed standing there, safe and unhurt, and he asked the Reed how he had managed to weather a storm, strong enough to blow down an Oak tree.

"Well," explained the Reed, "I behave very differently from an Oak tree. Instead of being stiff and unbending, and relying on my strength, as you do, I relax and bend with the storm, as I know I am not strong enough to resist it; and so I am not harmed."

Moral

You can often do better by giving way to other people than by opposing them.

The Horse and the Ass

The Horse and the Ass

A HORSE, wearing his great war saddle, came thundering and neighing down a mountain path. Presently he came to a heavily laden Ass going quietly in the same direction. The Horse immediately shouted to him in a proud and haughty voice to get out of his way, or he would trample him to death! The poor frightened Ass at once did as he was asked, and the Horse went on his way.

Soon after this the Horse was shot in the eye during a battle, which made him useless as a war horse, so he was sold to a carrier. The Ass, meeting him, exclaimed: "Oh! It's you, is it? I always thought that pride of yours would have a fall one day!"

Moral

Pride goes before a fall.

The Angler and the Little Fish

The Angler and the Little Fish

A FISHERMAN, after a hard day's work, caught one small perch, which he was taking off the hook to put into his basket, when it spoke to him, begging him to throw it back into the river again. The Man asked it why he should do such a thing.

"Well," said the Fish, "at the moment I am young and small and not nearly as worth your while to keep as I shall be when I have grown bigger!"

"That may be," replied the Man, "but I am not such a fool as to give up a certainty for an uncertainty!"

Moral

No time like the present.

The Ant and the Grasshopper

The Ant and the Grasshopper

ONE winter day a number of Ants were busy airing their store of corn in little heaps outside the door of their home.

A Grasshopper, who had managed to survive from the summer before, passed by, and being starved with cold and hunger, went up to the Ants and begged them for just one grain of corn to relieve his hunger. One of the Ants looked at him in surprise, and asked him how he had spent the time in the summer if he had not laid in stores for the winter as they had done.

"Oh! I had a lovely time drinking and singing and dancing," said the Grasshopper, "and I'm afraid I never thought of the winter!"

"In that case," said the Ant, "I'm sorry, but I can't keep you. Those who won't work in the summer must starve in the winter!"

Moral

Provide for the future.

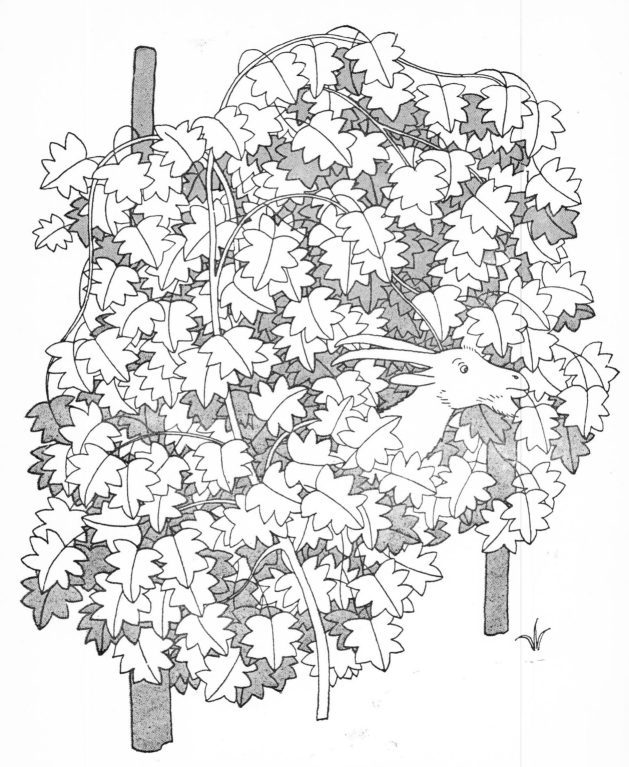

The Goat and the Vine

The Goat and the Vine

A HUNTED Goat took refuge in a vineyard, and lay there hidden by the Vine. As soon as he thought he was safe he started to eat the vine leaves, but the movement, or rustling of the leaves, attracted the huntsmen, and the Goat was discovered and killed. As he died he realized that his punishment was just, because he had injured the thing that had protected him.

Moral

It is a bad fault to be ungrateful

The Kite, the Frog, and the Mouse

The Kite, the Frog, and the Mouse

THERE was great rivalry between the Mouse and the Frog as to who should be master of the Fen. The Mouse was more crafty, but the Frog was stronger, and in the end challenged the Mouse to battle. They had both armed themselves with a bulrush for a spear, and started to fight, when a Kite, flying in the air, saw them. They were both so intent on each other that they did not see the Kite, who flew down and carried the two fighters off in her claws.

Moral

People who quarrel among themselves may easily find themselves in trouble.

PRINTED IN ROMANIA